This book belongs to:

Kevin McMaster

THE BRASS BAND ROBBERY

Written & Illustrated by John Patience

DERRYDALE BOOKS
New York
© Fern Hollow Productions Ltd:
Peter Haddock Ltd., U.K.
This 1984 edition is published by Derrydale Books,
distributed by Crown Publishers, Inc.
Printed in Italy.
ISBN 0-517-427907

One morning a large wooden crate arrived on the freight
train at Fern Hollow station. It was addressed to Lord
Trundle and marked "FRAGILE".
"I wonder what it can be?" said old Stripey, the Porter.
"I don't know," replied Mr. Twinkle, the Station Master.
"But I'd better telephone Lord Trundle to let him know
it's arrived."

When he heard the news, Lord Trundle was very excited and rushed down to the railroad station in his car. "Ah, at last!" he cried, looking at the great big wooden crate. "I've been waiting for this to arrive for weeks."

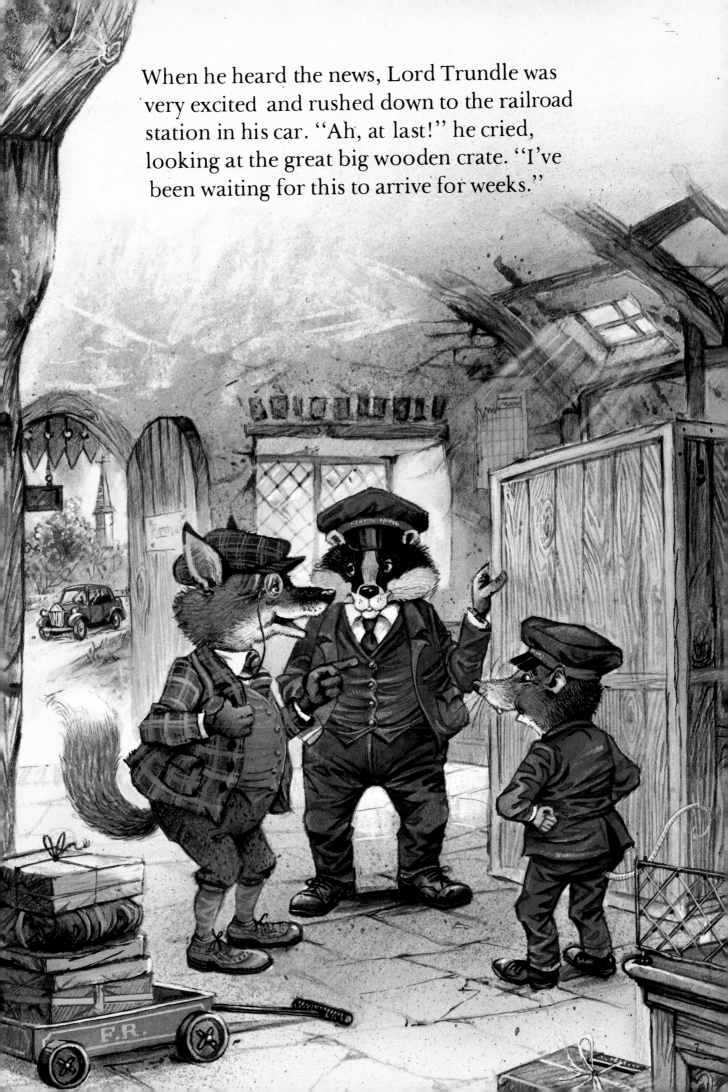

The crate was much too big to go inside Lord Trundle's car, so old Stripey and Mr. Twinkle helped him to tie it on to the roof rack, then away went the car, bouncing and rattling down the road.

The next day
Lord Trundle held
a meeting at Trundleberry Manor.
"As you all know," he began. "May Day isn't far away
now, and I wanted to do something really special in the
way of celebrations, so I've bought these!"
Lord Trundle pointed to the great big wooden crate.
"Musical instruments," he went on. "Fern Hollow is
going to have a brass band!"

Everyone had been given a musical instrument and the band had begun to practice, when suddenly the door burst open and in walked Snitch and Snatch. No one had invited them because they were always causing trouble. The two sneaky weasles had been peeping through the keyhole and had decided that they wanted to join the band.

"Give me the big drum," said Snatch.
"I'll have the sousaphone," said Snitch.
"I'm afraid there are only two triangles left," said Lord
Trundle politely.
"We don't want your silly triangles!" screamed Snitch.
"And what's more, if we can't have the drum and
sousaphone, then you won't have them for long either!"
And off they went, slamming the door behind them.

That night, Snitch and Snatch broke into Trundleberry
Manor intending to steal the drum and sousaphone. But as
Snitch was carrying the drum down the steps in front of
the Manor, it slipped out of his hands.
BOOM BOOM BOOM
it went as it bounced down the steps.

The noise woke Lord Trundle, who jumped out of bed and looked out of his window, just in time to see the two weasles running away with the musical instruments. Quickly Lord Trundle telephoned Fern Hollow Police Station.

Policeman Hoppit arrived a few minutes later, looking slightly out of breath from pedaling his bicycle so fast. "Don't worry, Lord Trundle," he panted. "We'll soon track the villains down. Which way did they go?"

Lord Trundle pointed
out the direction which
Snitch and Snatch had taken,
and followed P.C. Hoppit as the
Policeman raced off in pursuit.

"There they are," cried P.C. Hoppit. "Down on the river bank. We've got them now—they'll never be able to swim all the way across the Ferny with the drum and sousaphone!"

But the wily weasles had a plan. They
pushed the big drum out into the river
and jumped on top. Then Snitch began
to paddle with a stick, while Snatch held
onto the sousaphone.

Soon the weasles were halfway across
the river leaving Lord Trundle and P.C.
Hoppit standing helplessly on the bank.

It looked very much like Snitch and Snatch were going to get away, but suddenly the drum became caught in a strong current, and was swept away down river.

The terrified weasles clung onto the drum for all they were worth, but it was no use, because they were quickly swept over the waterfalls. Luckily for them, Mr. Whirlygill, the Ferryman, was watching and was able to drag them both out.

As a punishment P.C. Hoppit locked
Snitch and Snatch up in Fern Hollow
Police Station for a few days where they
missed all the May Day fun.
Lord Trundle's brass band was, of course,
a great success. They paraded around the
streets of Fern Hollow all afternoon,
before at last they stopped for a well-
deserved rest at the Jolly Vole,
where Mr. Crackleberry supplied
everyone with orange juice
and sandwiches!

Fern Hollow

MR CHIPS'S HOUSE

MR WILLOWBANK'S
COBBLERS SHOP

MR CROAKER'S WATERMILL

STRIPEY'S HOUSE

SCHOOL

THE JOLLY VOLE
HOTEL

RIVER FERNY

MR ACORN'S
BAKERY

MR RUSTY'S HOUSE

MR PRICKLES'S HOUSE

POST OFFICE

BORIS BLINKS'S
BOOKSHOP

MR TWINKLE'S
HOUSE

MR TUTTLEEBEE'S
SHOP

MR THIMBLE'S
TAILORS SHOP

WINDYWOOD